Mr. Neatolini

My dad likes to vacuum the grass!

Nellie Neatolini

While she was cleaning, Aunt Nellie Neatolini almost threw out my cousin Dini.

Mrs. Neatolini

My mom irons her linguini.

And then there's me, Angelina Neatolini. I like to roll in the dirt whenever I can.

The HOUSE at the end of Ladybug Lane

by Elise Primavera
illustrated by Valeria Docampo

robin corey books

New York

All rights reserved. Published in the United States by Robin Corey Books, an imprint of Random House Children's Books,
a division of Random House, Inc., 1745 Broadway, New York, NY 10019.

Robin Corey Books and the colophon are trademarks of Random House, Inc.

Visit us on the Web!
www.randomhouse.com/kids
RobinCoreyBooks.com

Educators and librarians, for a variety of teaching tools, visit us at www.randomhouse.com/teachers

Library of Congress Cataloging-in-Publication Data
Primavera, Elise.
The House at the End of Ladybug Lane / by Elise Primavera; illustrations by Valeria Docampo. — 1st ed.
p. cm.
Summary: Angelina Neatolini's wish for a pet, denied by her family on the grounds that pets are too messy, is overheard by a
hard-of-hearing ladybug, who fills their tidy new home with assorted pests.
ISBN 978-0-375-85584-9 (hardcover) — ISBN 978-0-375-95584-6 (Gibraltar library binding) [1. Orderliness—Fiction.
2. Family life—Fiction. 3. Insects—Fiction. 4. Moving, Household—Fiction. 5. Hearing impaired—Fiction.
6. Wishes—Fiction.] I. Docampo, Valeria. ill. II. Title.
PZ7.P9354Hou 2012   [E]—dc22   2010031850

The text of this book is set in Belucian.
The illustrations were rendered in gouache on paper.

MANUFACTURED IN MALAYSIA

10 9 8 7 6 5 4 3 2 1

First Edition

For Petra Mathers, who will always be my neatest friend
—E.P.

For lending me your hands and for lending me your stars,
thank you so very much, Virginia and Dominique!
—V.D.

It was the house at the end of Ladybug Lane, and to the Neatolinis it was a dream come true.

They had left city life behind.

"Good riddance!" said Mr. Neatolini. "Why, it made my clothes wrinkly just to walk out the door!"

"That city was not neat," said Mrs. Neatolini.

When they moved to the house at the end of Ladybug Lane, the Neatolinis threw everything inside away to get rid of the clutter. They shampooed the walls and the floors till they were squeaky-clean.

Then they went outside and vacuumed the grass and polished the flowers.

Now the house at the end of Ladybug Lane was the perfect place for all the Neatolinis . . .

. . . all except one.

Angelina was the only Neatolini who was not neat.
Her parents dressed her up in starchy pressed pants and
tried to hold her hair down with perfect tight bows.

But five minutes later, Angelina was always wrinkly and rumpled and covered in crumbs.

Not only that, she constantly pestered her parents to buy her a pet.

"A pet?" the Neatolinis said. "Pets are not neat!"

"Could I please have a dog, or a cat, or a gerbil? Some lovebirds?
A parrot? How about a chicken, an iguana, or maybe some raccoons?"

"Pets are messy!" her parents said.

"A sand crab? A jellyfish?" Angelina said hopefully.

"Stop being a PEST!" Her parents stomped off to their neat room.
"We'll see you in the morning at six-twenty-three!"

Angelina gazed out the window sadly, and when she saw the first star,
she whispered, "I wish I had a pet."

"No problem," a tiny voice said.

A ladybug stood alone on the sill. She twirled around three times to the right and three times to the left. "Abracadabra, ta-da! Give this kid a pest!"

"PET!" yelled Angelina.

Right away the pest came. He went straight to the kitchen and emptied his bag. Out tumbled magical things like powdered sky, tincture of marigold, ground-up forget-me-nots, and distilled eye of daydream.

He preheated the oven to 350 degrees and started at once to sift and to stir. He silently mixed everything into a batter, which sloshed out of bowls and plopped onto the floor.

He made a horrible mess! But soon cookies and cakes, fritters and pies flew out of the oven and covered the counters and shelves.

The ladybug grinned. "This pest has been looking for ages for just the right nest!"

"But I wanted a *pet,* not a pest!" Angelina stomped her foot.

"What?" said the ladybug, cupping an ear. "I'm sorry, my dear, but I couldn't quite hear."

Angelina said louder, "I wish I had a nice little minnow, a sparrow, or perhaps some sardines?"

"No problem," said the ladybug. "Abracadabra, ta-da! Give this kid some carpenter bees!"

The bees whooshed in through a window and got right to work building couches and chairs.

"But you don't *understand*!" Angelina cried. "I'd like a pet turtle, a tuna, or maybe a non-biting viper!"

"Excellent idea!" said the ladybug. "Abracadabra, ta-da! Give this kid a pink widow spider!"

A large, hairy pink spider crawled in through the window and made lacy white curtains. She made comfy striped cushions and squishy plaid pillows—and for the floors, she made rugs.

The ladybug said proudly, "She's my *best* weaving bug."

"You're not hearing my wishes!" Angelina said, pouting. "By any chance, do you think I might have a pet poodle?"

"No problem," replied the ladybug. "Abracadabra, ta-da! Give this kid one dozen doodles!"

The doodlebugs marched in and covered the walls with colors like parakeet yellow, merry pink, and Christmas red. They painted all the trim cornflower blue.

Angelina gave up and snuggled next to the pest, who offered her a chrysanthemum cupcake.

The night was now over.

The first rays of sun shone through the lace curtains and showed off all the bugs' work.

"Pretty!" Angelina declared. Much to her surprise, the house at the end of Ladybug Lane was the perfect place to be.

"Look at the time!" said the ladybug. "Why, it's six-twenty-three!"

"Six-twenty-three?!" Angelina braced herself for what would come next.

The Neatolinis emerged from their bedroom; their eyes blinked and their mouths gaped.

At the top of their lungs they both screamed, "Our house is not neat! GET RID OF THESE PESTS!!!!!!!"

For the first time all night, the ladybug could hear perfectly.

"No problem," she said. "Abracadabra, ta-da!" And—*poof!*— she disappeared.

The other bugs scattered, except for the pest.

"Oh, please let him stay," Angelina begged. "Try his cakes, taste his cookies."

So her parents nibbled a cookie and tasted a cake, a blueberry fritter, and a prune Danish or two.

"Yummy," they said, then gobbled the cranberry turnovers and a pineapple cobbler.

The Neatolinis flopped onto a polka-dot couch.

"Don't you just love the house and these rooms now?" Angelina asked.

"Why, it sparkles, it dazzles!" the Neatolinis said with their mouths full, having no idea that everything they were eating was loaded with magic.

By 6:53 the Neatolinis had agreed to let the pest stay!

No, Angelina still was not neat, but now her parents didn't want to change her one bit. They all lived happily ever after with the pest in the house at the end of Ladybug Lane.

For Angelina Neatolini,
it was a dream come true.

I come from a long line of extremely neat people:

Nathaniel Neatolini

My great-great-great-great-
great-grandfather Nathaniel Neatolini
invented the garbage can.

Nina Neatolini

My great-great-great-grandmother
Nina Neatolini whitewashed the barn
as well as all the brown cows once a year.

Pioneer Neatolini

The Pioneer Neatolinis settled the West
and covered their covered wagons
to keep the dust off.